A Birthday Surprise

Story by:
Margaret Ann Hughes

Lyrics by:
Mark Shumate

Music Composed by:
George Wilkins

Illustrated by:

Russell Hicks	Fay Whitemountain
Theresa Mazurek	Su-Zan
Douglas McCarthy	Lisa Souza
Allyn Conley	Julie Ann Armstrong
Lorann Downer	Pat Ventura
Rivka	Julie Zakowski

This Book Belongs To:

Use this symbol to match book and cassette.

Once upon a time, actually not so long ago, my special day began…with Hector.

Hector wanted to know when I had my last birthday, but I couldn't remember.

I didn't know it at the time, but that's when Hector decided that it had been too long since I had a real birthday. So off he waddled to plan a special birthday party surprise just for me.

Hector began making invitations to the surprise party right away. He cut and pasted the invitations and put them in envelopes. Then he found Nigel, the Town Crier, and asked him to help deliver the invitations.

Hector and Nigel went door to door and left an
invitation in each mailbox. Then, as they walked
by the Town Square, Nigel announced the surprise
party to everyone in the Fairy Tale Township.

All my fairy tale friends were invited to the party–Little Red Riding Hood, Cinderella, Jack, Rumpelstiltskin, Briar Rose, Pembroke the Frog Prince, Leonard the Tortoise, Skip the Hare and the Three Bears…

Warren the Wolf was certain he wouldn't be invited. So Warren planned a surprise of his own–to steal the birthday presents.

Meanwhile, the rest of the Township planned their surprise for me.

They all worked for many days–baking, sewing, making things–until the day of my party finally arrived. Everyone in the Township met early in the clearing of the Ever-Green Woods. There was still a lot to do.

Hector was supposed to bring me to the Ever-Green Woods at noon for the big surprise party. In the meantime, he kept me busy all morning long so I wouldn't discover his special secret.

I told Hector one story after another, and all the while in the Ever-Green Woods…

…everyone was busy decorating!

"A Stupendous Birthday Party"

Now we'll have a birthday party.
We'll make everything just right.
And our special guest of honor
Will be bursting with delight.

A stupendous birthday party
Will be magic, guaranteed.
What a fine idea to have one.
It's exactly what we need.

At the party we'll have presents.
We'll have food and songs and games.
We'll wear funny party hats
And we'll use funny, funny names.

We'll be sure the decorations
Are the finest we can make.
And to top things off completely–
A delicious birthday cake.

It's not long until they'll be here.
This is going to be some fun.
Let's find a place to hide.
Someone watch for when they come.

When our birthday guest just stands there
And cannot believe her eyes,
We'll start singing, "Happy Birthday,"
But first we'll shout, "Surprise!"

They're up to something.
Something is going on.
Though they won't say,
I know that something's going on.

Then when everything was ready, the
Giant took all the presents and hid them by
the old oak tree, as a final
surprise.

By this time, I had told Hector practically every
story I could think of.

When Hector learned it was almost noon, he
became quite excited about taking a walk. It was
all I could do to keep up with him.

It wasn't long before we reached the clearing in the Ever-Green Woods. There, before me, was a picture I'll never forget. There were balloons, streamers, a big decorated cake, and best of all, there were my friends, together in one place.

Well, we had a wonderful time. We played all
kinds of party games, like "Pin the Tail on Papa
Bear." That was Baby Bear's idea. And we played
a guessing game with Rumpelstiltskin. Then we
ate lunch. And we finished with a beautiful
three-layered cake that the Little Red Hen
had baked.

Meanwhile, who do you suppose was watching us from behind the old oak tree? That's right! It was Warren the Wolf! When no one was looking, he stuffed all the presents into a large bag.

Then he tip-toed away, dragging the bag of gifts behind him. He left the bag beneath a bush. Then he hid behind a tree to watch the fun.

The Giant ran to the old oak tree to get the presents...but they weren't there!

Everyone was very upset. That's when I told them about the very special gift that each had already given me.

A gift need not be a present...

"The Gift Of You"

Please do not feel sad.
I do not feel bad.
This doesn't spoil
The joyous day I've had.

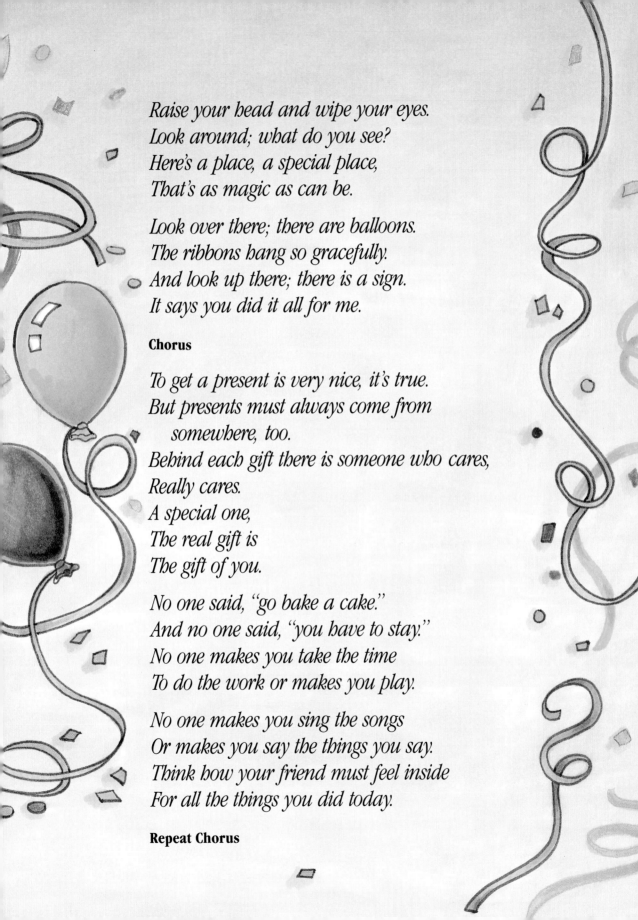

Raise your head and wipe your eyes.
Look around; what do you see?
Here's a place, a special place,
That's as magic as can be.

Look over there; there are balloons.
The ribbons hang so gracefully.
And look up there; there is a sign.
It says you did it all for me.

Chorus

To get a present is very nice, it's true.
But presents must always come from
    somewhere, too.
Behind each gift there is someone who cares,
Really cares.
A special one,
The real gift is
The gift of you.

No one said, "go bake a cake."
And no one said, "you have to stay."
No one makes you take the time
To do the work or makes you play.

No one makes you sing the songs
Or makes you say the things you say.
Think how your friend must feel inside
For all the things you did today.

Repeat Chorus

Then carefully the Fairy Godmother took a little something from everyone–a piece of thread, a bit of lace, a satin ribbon. And with the wave of her wand…she magically created the most beautiful bonnet and collar I had ever seen.

Everyone felt much better and we had such a good time together. But Warren the Wolf just couldn't understand how everyone could be so happy.

Then Warren remembered the bag of gifts, but when he went back to the bush…the bag was gone!

Now it was Warren's turn to be disappointed.
Back at the clearing, another guest had just arrived.
It was Leonard the Tortoise, plodding along in his
usual slow, but steady, pace.

Leonard was dragging a bag full of presents.

Meanwhile, Warren the Wolf was still searching every bush in the area, trying to find the bag of presents. He never discovered that Leonard the Tortoise had found it.

Poor Warren! If only he had known–the invitation to the party had been in his mailbox all along.

Oh, it was a wonderful birthday party, and thank you for sharing it with me all over again. It's so nice to remember.

And we all lived happily ever after.